For Dad,
the original noise maker

SQUEAK !

Mi

Re

Do

SOAP

RAT and ROACH

ROCK ON!

SQUEAK !

SQUEAK !

La

La

by
David
Covell

VIKING
An Imprint of Penguin Group (USA) Inc.

Here is Rat with his junkyard band getting ready for the Big City Jam.

And this is Rat's best friend, Roach.
They like one another, like best friends do,
but they don't always like the same things.

"Roach, what's that thing you've got on?"

"Don't you like it? See how it sparkles? See how it shines? I made one for all of us in the band."

Now everyone knows rats are not fancy.
They'd rather be sloppy and grungy.

"Pssst, Rat.
We don't want
to dress up fancy."

"Yeah, we're a down
and dirty band."

There's only one thing Rat can do . . .

"Mmmmeeerrrrrrr,
errrrrrrrrgggggggg . . ."

"Aaaaaaaahhh,
eeeeeeeeeeee . . ."

It's on with the show. . . .

"Ladies and gentlemen! Cats and kitties! This is the night of the Big City Jam. Sweep out the cobwebs and turn on the spotlights for

THE RAT-A-TAT PACK and ROACH!"

"C'mon Roach, don't be shy.
Let's rock those cats right out of their seats."

"Rat! Close the curtain! I can't go on."

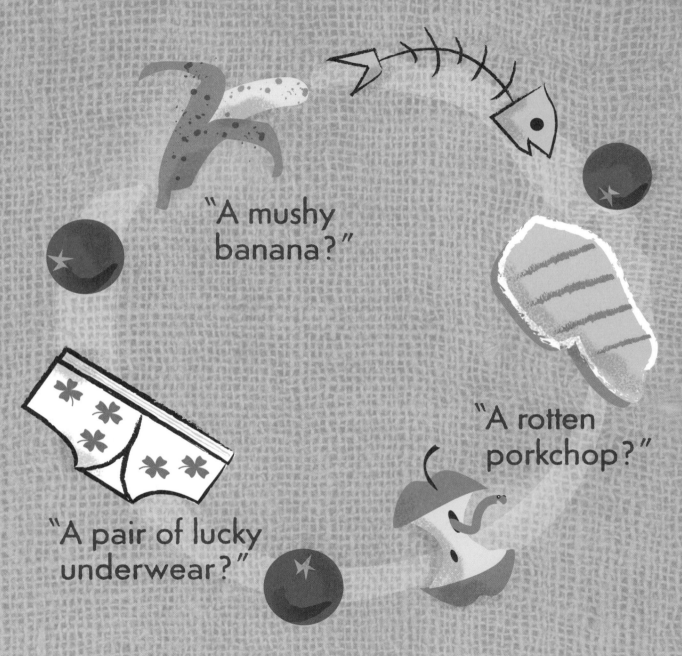

"Will you sing for a trashy treat?"

"A mushy banana?"

"A rotten porkchop?"

"A pair of lucky underwear?"

"Icky. Sticky. Stinky!
Rat, that's everything you like. Nothing for me."

"Roach, *please*! I'm on my knees.
Just open up and let it out!
Everyone is waiting."

"Don't you hear? I can't sing!
My sparkle's gone. I lost my shine.
**Now, quit
bugging me!**"

"Rat, you found
my shine!"

"I feel funny."

Two sounds so much better. ♪
Let's get the band together!

Three rats will rock you. On your feet!
C'mon Roach, give us the beat!

1-2-3-4

Everyone up on

the dance floor!

"Congratulations, Roach. You didn't squeak!"

"Thank you, Rat, for playing along.
I didn't squeak with you by my side."

"Don't worry, Roach. You can count on me — even if we dress up fancy."

"Hey! My favorite shirt! Yowza. This one itches."

"Rat, you're a real star."
"Roach, I couldn't go on without you."

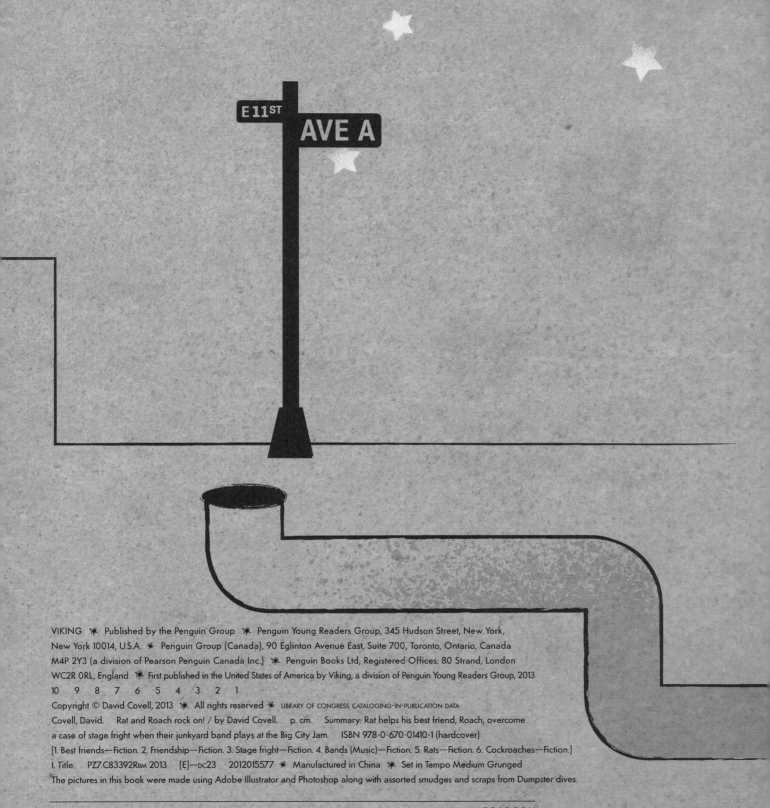

VIKING ✳ Published by the Penguin Group ✳ Penguin Young Readers Group, 345 Hudson Street, New York,
New York 10014, U.S.A. ✳ Penguin Group (Canada), 90 Eglinton Avenue East, Suite 700, Toronto, Ontario, Canada
M4P 2Y3 (a division of Pearson Penguin Canada Inc.) ✳ Penguin Books Ltd, Registered Offices: 80 Strand, London
WC2R 0RL, England ✳ First published in the United States of America by Viking, a division of Penguin Young Readers Group, 2013

10   9   8   7   6   5   4   3   2   1

Covell, David.   Rat and Roach rock on! / by David Covell.   p. cm.   Summary: Rat helps his best friend, Roach, overcome
a case of stage fright when their junkyard band plays at the Big City Jam.   ISBN 978-0-670-01410-1 (hardcover)
[1. Best friends—Fiction. 2. Friendship—Fiction. 3. Stage fright—Fiction. 4. Bands (Music)—Fiction. 5. Rats—Fiction. 6. Cockroaches—Fiction.]
I. Title.   PZ7.C83392Rbm 2013   [E]—dc23   2012015577 ✳ Manufactured in China ✳ Set in Tempo Medium Grunged
The pictures in this book were made using Adobe Illustrator and Photoshop along with assorted smudges and scraps from Dumpster dives.